Written by
Mark Thunder

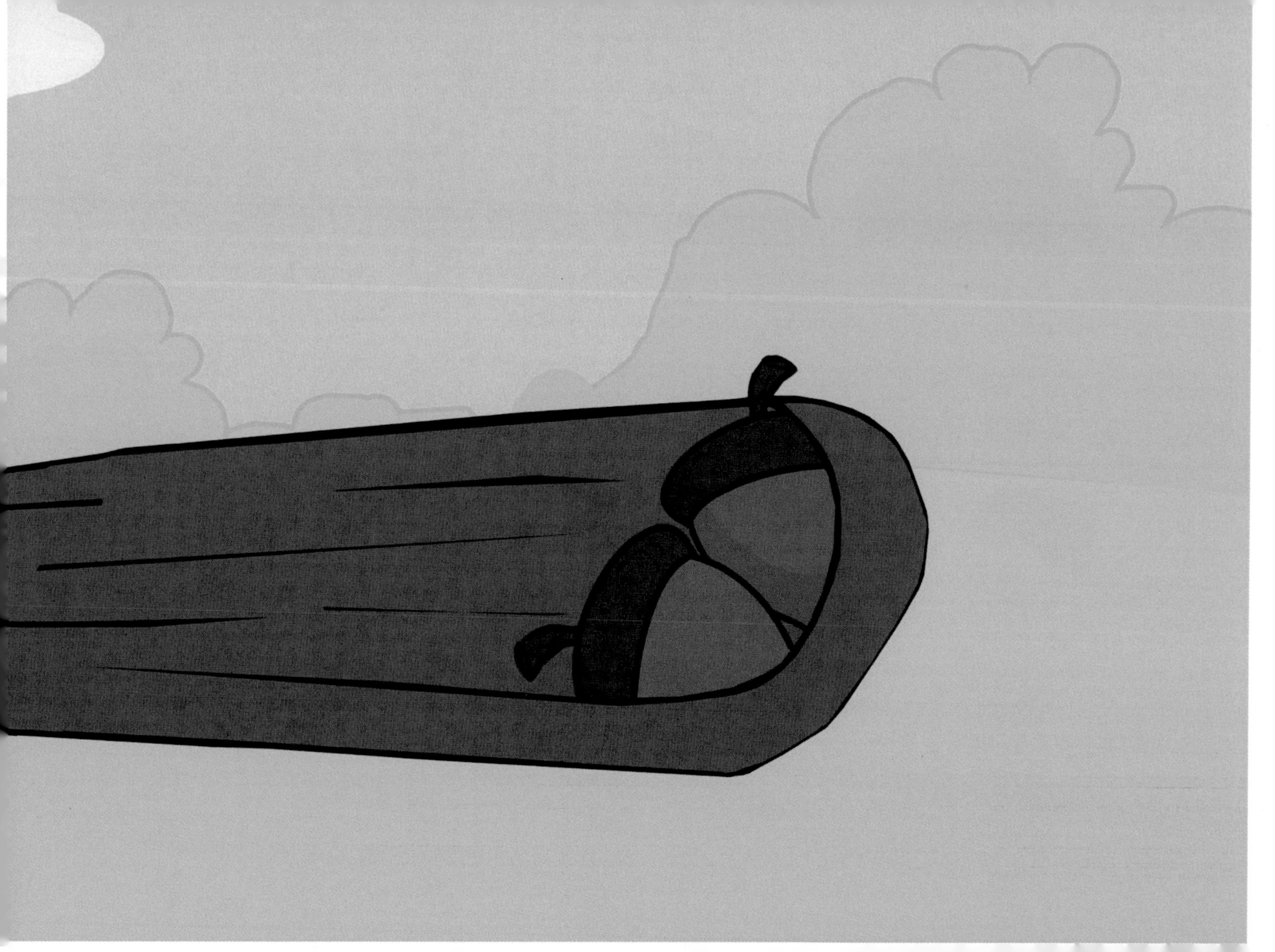

Made in the USA
Las Vegas, NV
20 November 2024

Mr. Eggplant
Written by Amalia Wu
Illustrated by Amalia Wu

ISBN: 9798345907290

With thanks to 乾奶奶 Lena for the inspiration.

Introduction

Eggplant

Mr. Eggplant is a worm from Planet WORMZ. Worms from Planet WORMZ have special powers, including flying and making their tails longer.

Sunshine

Miss Sunshine the Worm is Mr. Future Worm's daughter. She is very bright and quick to think and she has very good ideas too!

Strawberry

Miss Strawberry the Worm is very shy. She loves writing.

Future Worm

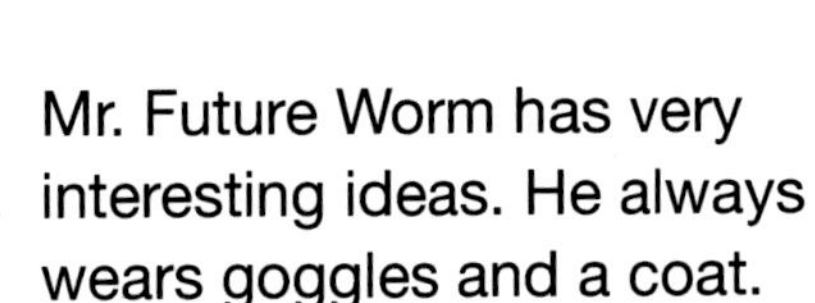

Mr. Future Worm has very interesting ideas. He always wears goggles and a coat. He can drive any vehicle.

Stylish Evil

Stylish Evil the Worm is really mean. He likes to play tricks and make deals.

One day, young Mr. Eggplant in Planet WORMZ took a walk in space far far away. But some astronauts were in the same place and accidentally stepped on poor Eggplant and he got carried to Earth!

When he landed, he said: “I have to get back home to Planet WORMZ in space far far away! But how? Hmmmmmmm.”

“I know,” said a voice. Eggplant turned around. “Who are you?” he asked.

“I am Miss Sunshine the Worm, and this is Miss Strawberry the Worm. We both came from Planet WORMZ, too.” said the voice. “Who are you?”

“I am Mr. Eggplant the Worm. Did you say you knew how I could get home to Planet WORMZ in space?” said Eggplant.

“Yes,” said Sunshine. “Would you like to know how?”

“Yes, please,” said Eggplant.

“Then follow us.” said Sunshine.

They crawled for a long time until they finally reached a big house. “Step inside.” said Sunshine.

When they went inside, Eggplant said: “Woooww, what is this place?”

Strawberry said: “Meet Mr. Future Worm!”

“Hi, Eggplant.” said Mr. Future Worm, “We have a rocket ship to take us back to Planet WORMZ, but we don’t have the code for it. The villain of the town, Stylish Evil the Worm, stole the the card with the code.”

Then he started to imitate Stylish Evil: “Wah ha ha ha! If you give me the magic pearl, I will give you the code for the rocket ship. Wah ha ha ha! And if you don’t, I will take one of you and make him or her my evil assistant forever! Wah ha ha ha ha!”

“Then I will go fight Stylish Evil and get that card back,” said Eggplant bravely.

All the worms in the house gasped.

“But- but- you you don’t have any weapons,” said Sunshine.

“Then I will make some,” said Eggplant.

“You can borrow my gold paint for your weapons,” offered Strawberry.

“Thank you,” said Eggplant. Eggplant made a golden sword from gold paint and a golden shield.

Future Worm showed Eggplant a map. He said: “This is where we are right now, in the middle of the town. You have to go to the edge of the town where Stylish Evil lives.”

Eggplant traveled to the edge of town. He saw a big black building and went into it. He saw Stylish Evil in the building.

“Sssssssoo, do you have the magic pearl or will you be my assistant forever?” asked Stylish Evil.

“Neither,” said Eggplant.

“So, will we fight then?” asked Stylish Evil snorting. “You have to get past my robotic worms first. Ha ha ha!”

Robotic worms started to fall from the ceiling. Eggplant used his shield to block off attacks, but he was soon surrounded by the robotic worms. So he got out his sword and slashed the ones on him.

Bang! Bang! Shing!

The robotic worms were either cut or lost power.

“It’s just you and me now, Stylish Evil.”

“Oh, really?” snickered Stylish Evil. He took out some fashionable worms with robotic parts. “Face all of us. Ha ha ha ha!”

Eggplant took out his sword and the worms started attacking with their tails, which got very long and sharp.

Eggplant blocked the attacks with his sword. He took a deep breath and jumped up to the ceiling. Eggplant started flying around; his tail had powers too! The tail grew longer and, with it, Eggplant picked up and attacked with his sword.

The worms quickly ran away!

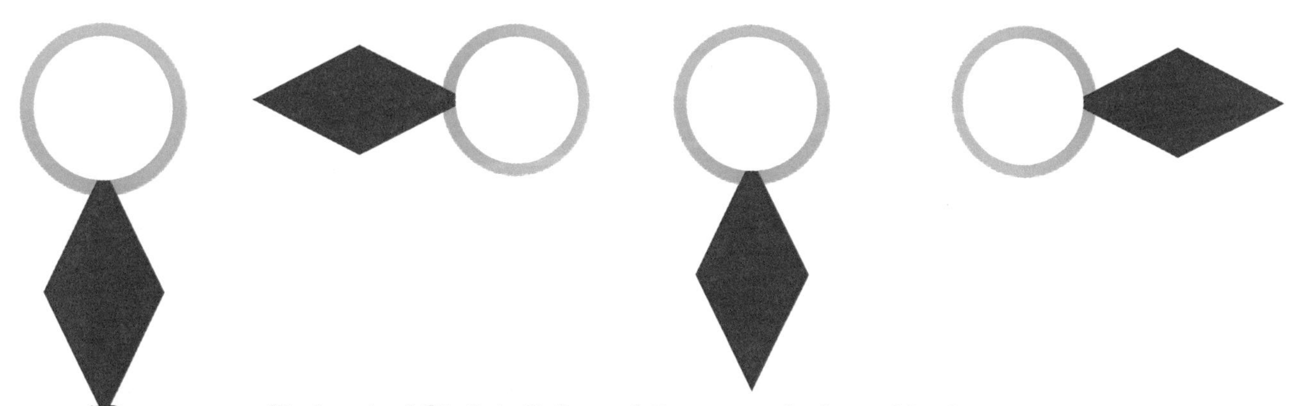

“Grrrrrrrrrrrrr!” shouted Stylish Evil, and threw neck ties with sharp edges.

Eggplant quickly dodged the neck ties. He flew towards Stylish Evil and attacked him!

Stylish Evil quickly got out of the way and said: “If you’re going to force me to get my new clothes dirty, I will have some fun with it!” Stylish Evil pulled out a sword! He used his sword to block Eggplant’s attacks!

Stylish Evil threw some neck ties. Eggplant caught one of them, and threw it towards Stylish Evil. Stylish Evil got trapped by his own weapon.

Eggplant pointed his sword at Stylish Evil: “Where is the card?” .

“In t-the top of the building on the top flo-floor,” answered Stylish Evil.

Mr. Eggplant tied Stylish Evil with a rope first and then climbed up the stairs to the top floor. He found the card because there were no other things there. He took it and flew to the center of the town where the house was.

"Congratulations!" said Future Worm. "You have got the code. Now let's launch the rocket ship!"

As they all went on to the rocket ship, Future Worm sat down at the pilot seat and put the code in to launch the rocket ship.

Beep beep boop!

The rocket ship blasted into space. They traveled for a long time. When the rocket ship finally landed, they climbed out of the rocket ship and crawled to the town and said goodbye to each other.

Eggplant told Future Worm, Sunshine, and Strawberry: “Thank you and I’m going to miss you!”

“You’re welcome,” said Strawberry.

“Here is a picture of us,” said Sunshine as she gave him a photo.

“Thank you and goodbye!” called out Eggplant.

Stop
Start

Eggplant arrived home and used his tail to knock on the door on the ground.

Eggplant's mom opened the door and said:"Dad, Eggplant is home!"

Eggplant's mom and dad rushed to him and hugged him.

"Oh, Eggplant, where were you?"

"I went to Earth, Ma," said Eggplant. "I made some friends. Here is a photograph of them."

"Was it scary, dear?" asked Eggplant's mom.

"Oh no," said Eggplant. "But I did have to fight this evil worm named Stylish Evil. But overall it was nice! But there's nowhere like home!"

The End

Made in USA
San Jose, CA
14 August 2024

Made in the USA
Las Vegas, NV
20 November 2024